Setting the Turkeys Free

Written by **W. Nikola-Lisa**

Illustrated by **Ken Wilson-Max**

JUMP AT THE SUN / Hyperion Books for Children • New York

Come see!

My dog and I are making a turkey!

First I put my hand in paint.

Then I spread my fingers apart and press

my hand onto a big piece of paper.

When I lift my hand . . .

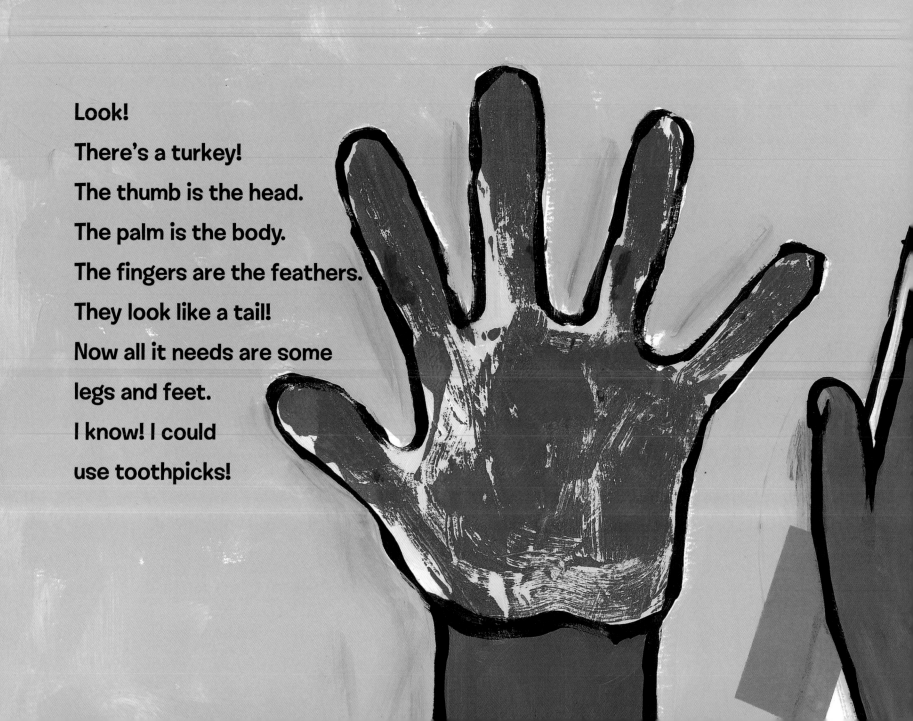

Look!

There's a turkey!

The thumb is the head.

The palm is the body.

The fingers are the feathers.

They look like a tail!

Now all it needs are some

legs and feet.

I know! I could

use toothpicks!

See? Now my turkey can walk!

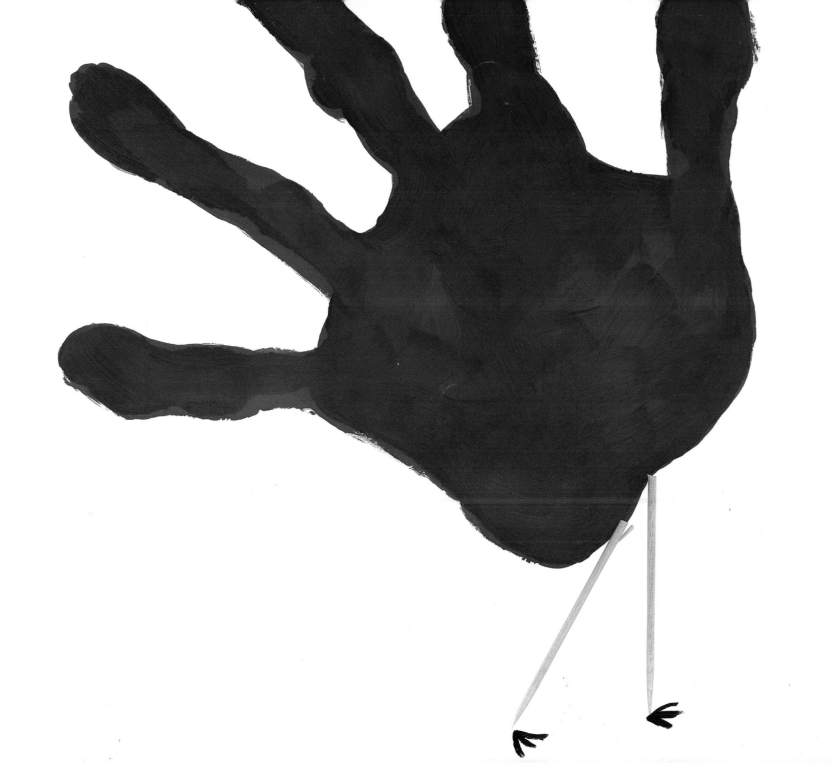

So I make another one—
and another, and another,
until I have lots of turkeys.

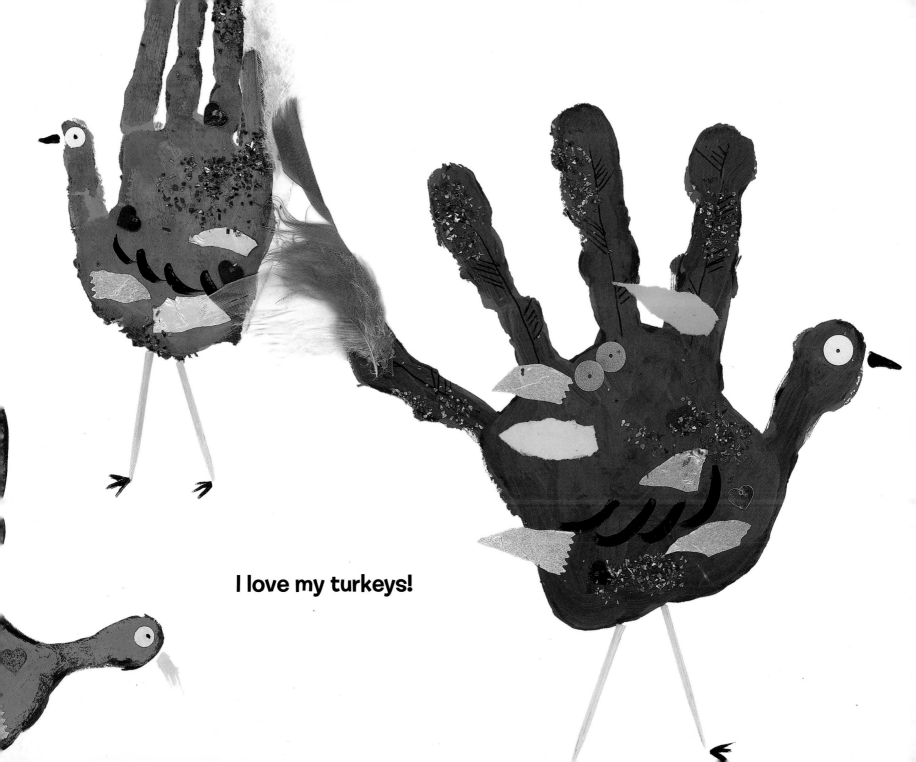

I love my turkeys!

To keep my turkeys safe, I make a pen out of Popsicle sticks.

Now they can run around in their own little yard.

Uh-oh! A storm is coming. And what's that I see?

Foxy the fox! Where'd *he* come from?

Go away, Foxy the fox!

You're frightening my turkeys!

GOBBLE-GOBBLE-GOBBLE!

Go away.

GOBBLE-GOBBLE!

Shoo!

Look! Foxy the fox can't believe his eyes.

The turkeys are hiding behind each other.

To him they look like one big fat turkey dinner!

No, Foxy the fox!

You can't have my turkeys!

But what should I do?

I know!

I make a fist, smear it in the paint,

and press it onto the paper—

right in front of Foxy the fox!

Oh, no! Foxy the fox is climbing over the rock!

I have to save my turkeys!

Quickly, I unlock the gate and push it open,

setting the turkeys free.

Now there's not a turkey in sight.

Ha! Take that, you mean old fox.

There will be no turkey dinner for you today!

But now I miss my turkeys.

So I cover the rock with grass
and put little pieces of corn on
the ground inside the turkey pen,
and hope that someday my
turkeys will come home to me.

And they do!

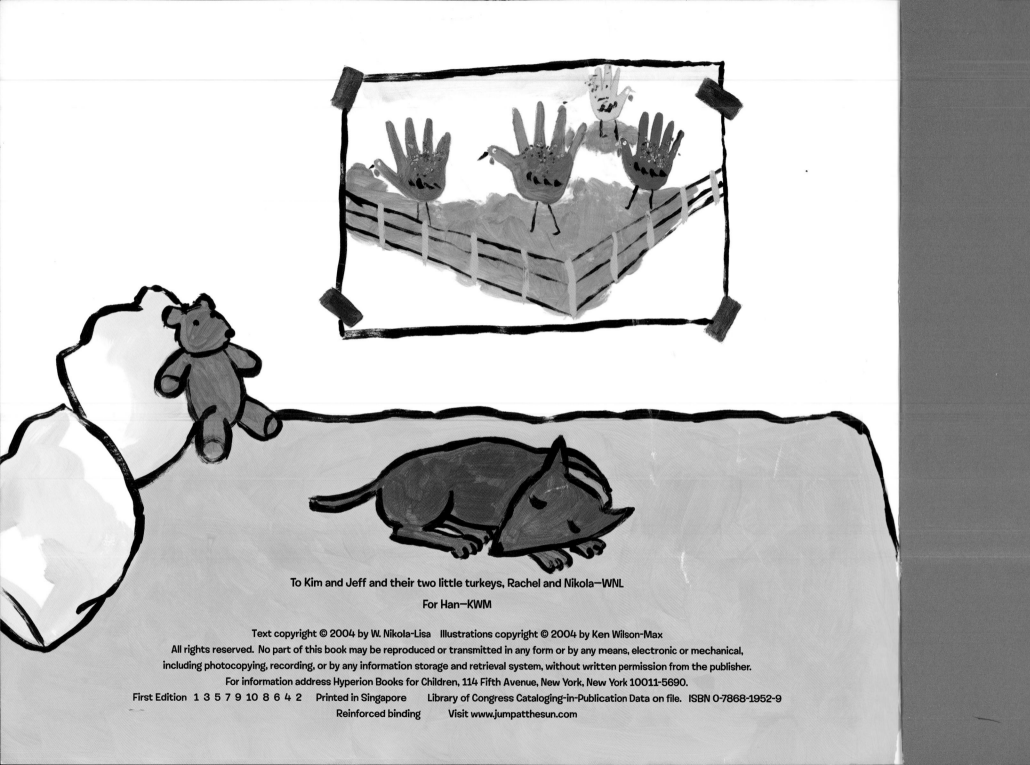

To Kim and Jeff and their two little turkeys, Rachel and Nikola—WNL

For Han—KWM

Text copyright © 2004 by W. Nikola-Lisa   Illustrations copyright © 2004 by Ken Wilson-Max
For information address Hyperion Books for Children, 114 Fifth Avenue, New York, New York 10011-5690.

First Edition 1 3 5 7 9 10 8 6 4 2   Printed in Singapore   Library of Congress Cataloging-in-Publication Data on file. ISBN 0-7868-1952-9
Reinforced binding   Visit www.jumpatthesun.com

And they do!

To Kim and Jeff and their two little turkeys, Rachel and Nikola—WNL

For Han—KWM

Text copyright © 2004 by W. Nikola-Lisa   Illustrations copyright © 2004 by Ken Wilson-Max

For information address Hyperion Books for Children, 114 Fifth Avenue, New York, New York 10011-5690.

First Edition 1 3 5 7 9 10 8 6 4 2   Printed in Singapore   Library of Congress Cataloging-in-Publication Data on file. ISBN 0-7868-1952-9

Reinforced binding   Visit www.jumpatthesun.com